THE GREAT
PEACE MARCH

To all the brave and loving
peace activists who have gone
before us, those yet to come,
and those of us here in this
moment on the Great Peace March
—H. N.

For Matt—with love
—L. D.

If you would like to order a recording of Holly Near singing
"The Great Peace March," please call 1-800-887-7664, or
write to Redwood Cultural Work, P. O. Box 10408, Oakland, CA 94610.

Words and music © 1986 Hereford Music
Illustrations copyright © 1993 by Lisa Desimini
All rights reserved, including the right to reproduce
this book or portions thereof in any form.
Published by Henry Holt and Company, Inc.,
115 West 18th Street, New York, New York 10011.
Published simultaneously in Canada by Fitzhenry & Whiteside Ltd.,
91 Granton Drive, Richmond Hill, Ontario L4B 2N5.

Library of Congress Cataloging-in-Publication Data
Near, Holly.
The great peace march / by Holly Near; paintings by Lisa Desimini.
Summary: An illustrated version of a song celebrating the
brotherhood of humanity and the possibility of world peace.
ISBN 0-8050-1941-3
I. Children's songs—Texts. [1. Peace—Songs and music.
2. Songs.] I. Desimini, Lisa, ill. II. Title.
PZ8.3.N317Gr 1993   782.42164'0268—dc20   92-25170

Printed in the United States of America
on acid-free paper. ∞

1 3 5 7 9 10 8 6 4 2
First edition

THE GREAT PEACE MARCH

By Holly Near ❖ Paintings by Lisa Desimini

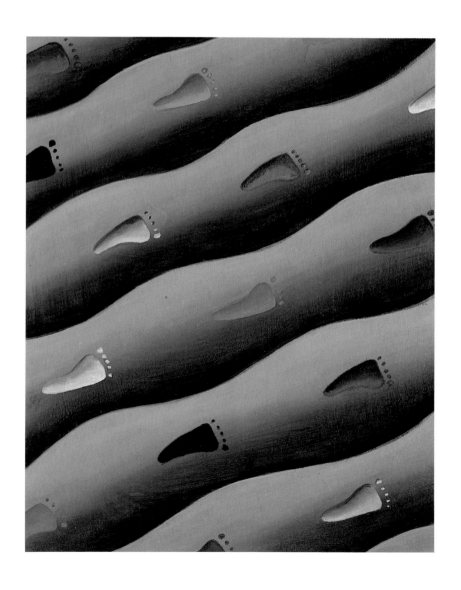

Henry Holt and Company ✦ New York

Ancient eyes are watching in the night,
The stars come out to guide the way.

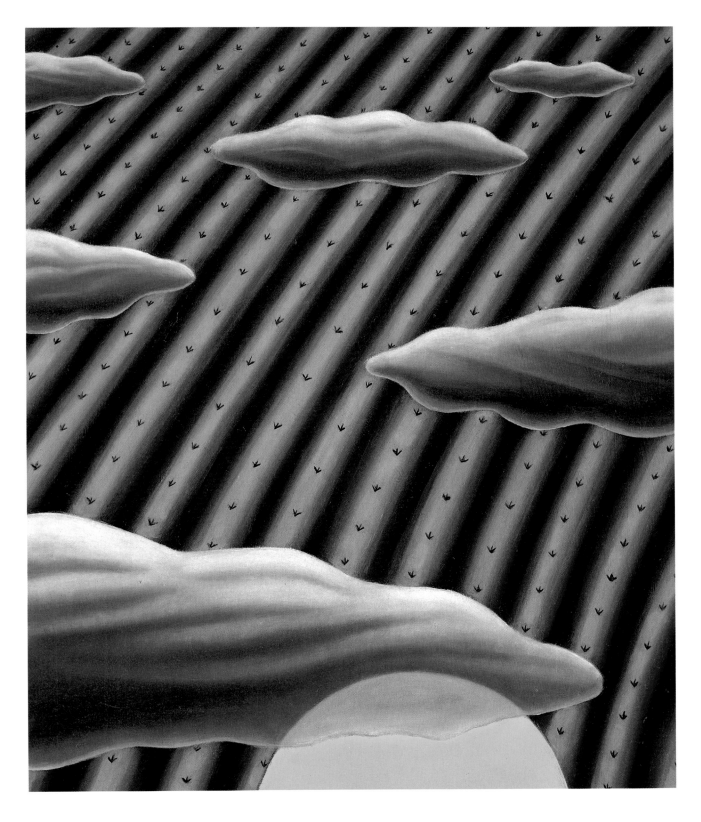

The sun still shines despite the clouds,
And the dawn is dusk is dawn is dusk is day.

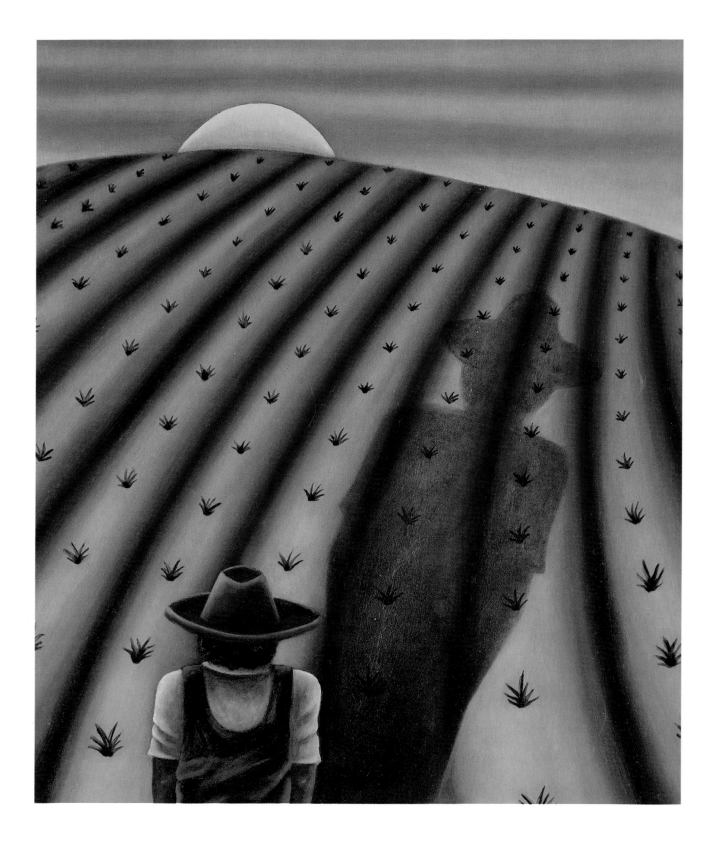

Farmers rise and dream to feed the world,

The world awakes to feed the heart.

Hearts beat while a thousand flags are waving,

And the farmer sees a dream has played a part.

Are you black like night

or red like clay?

Are you gold like sun

or brown like earth?

Gray like mist

or white like moon?

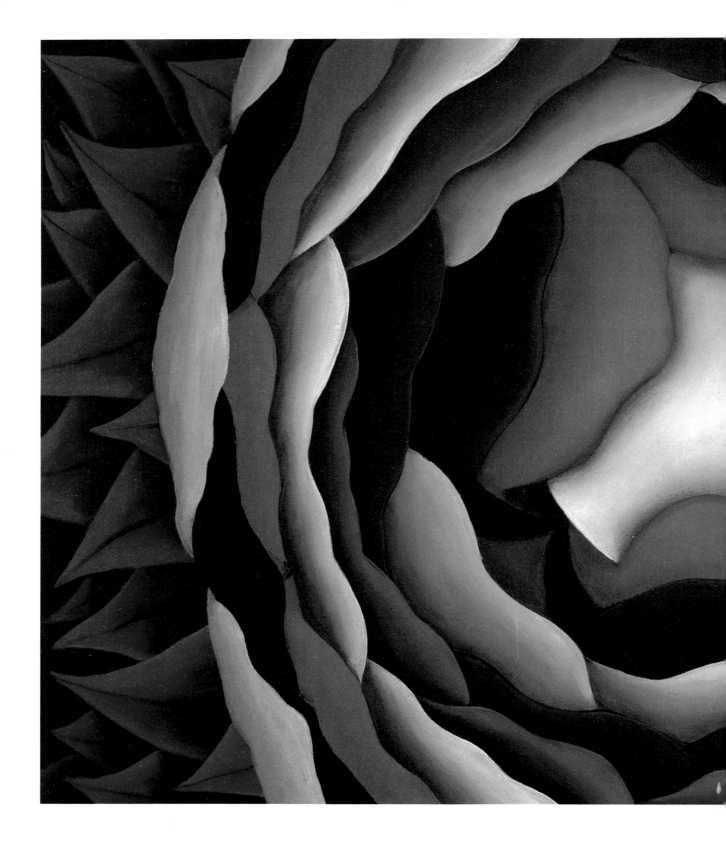

My love for you is the reason for my birth.

Peace can start with just one heart,

From a small step to leaps and bounds.

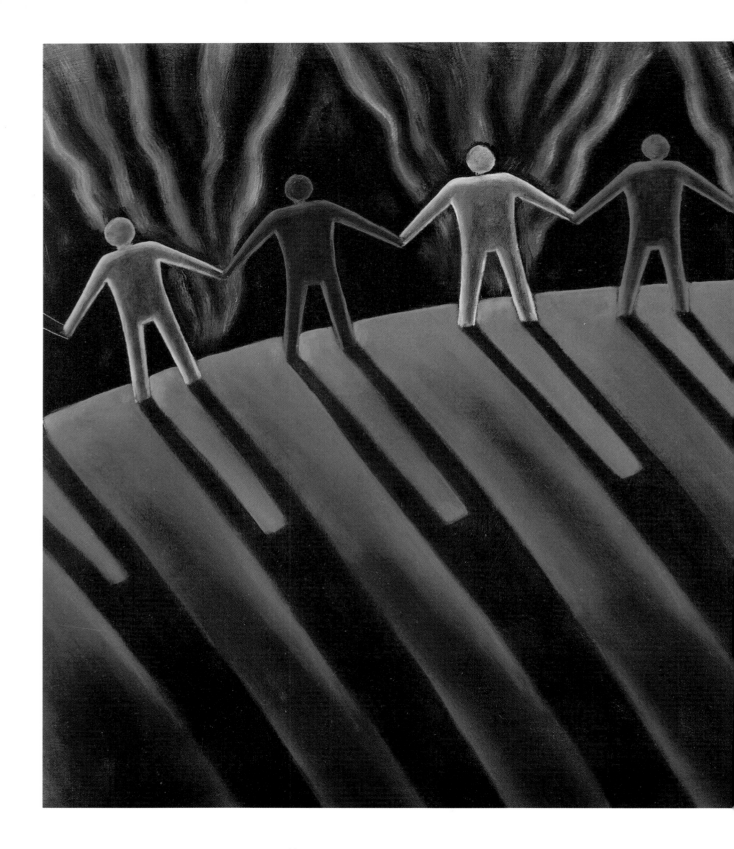

A walk becomes a race for time,

And a brave child calls out from the crowd...

We will have peace, we will because we must,

We must because we cherish life;

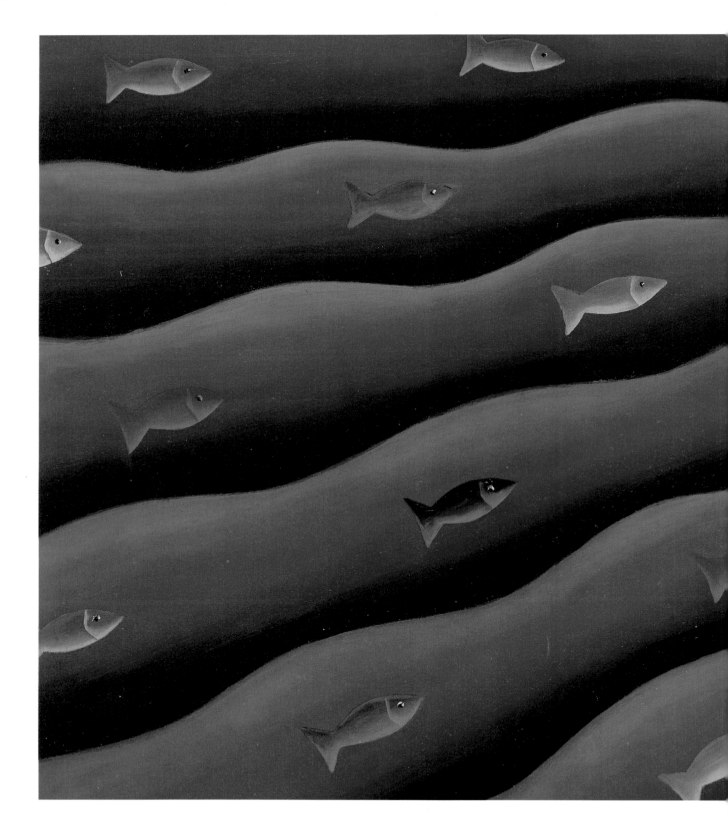

And believe it or not, as daring as it may seem,

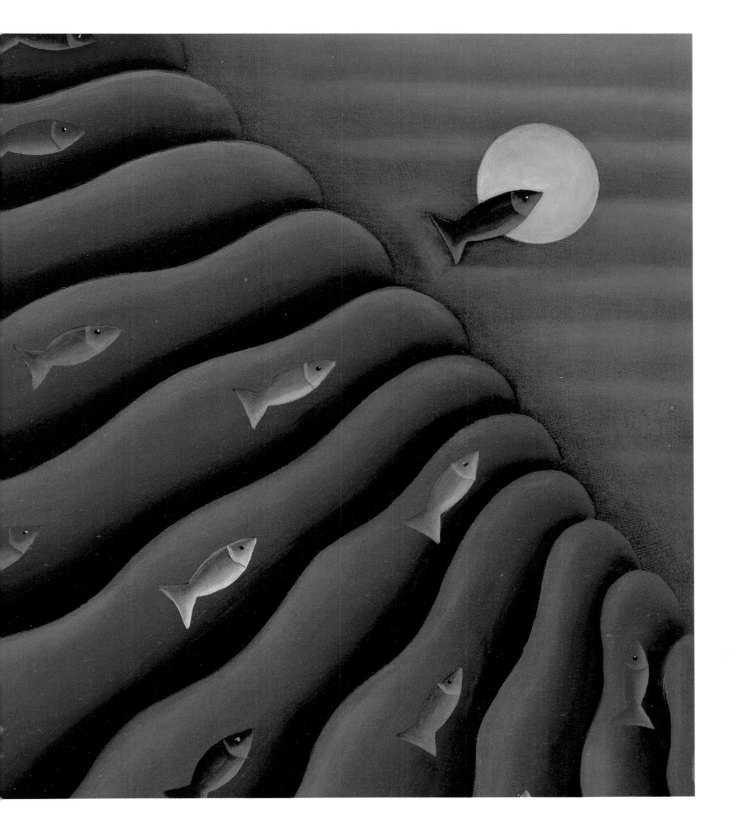

It is not an empty dream

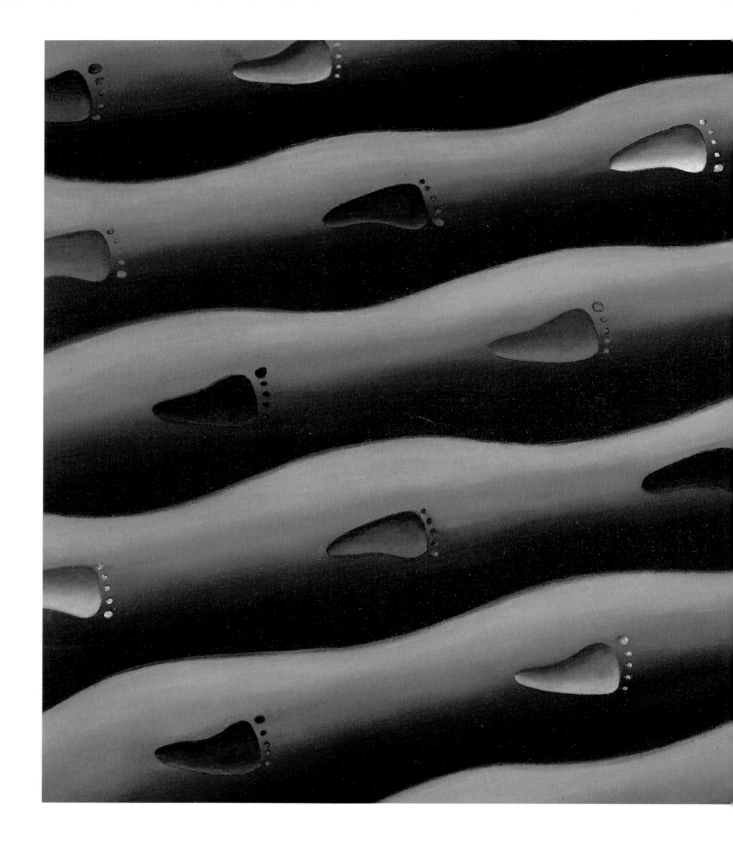

To walk in a powerful path,

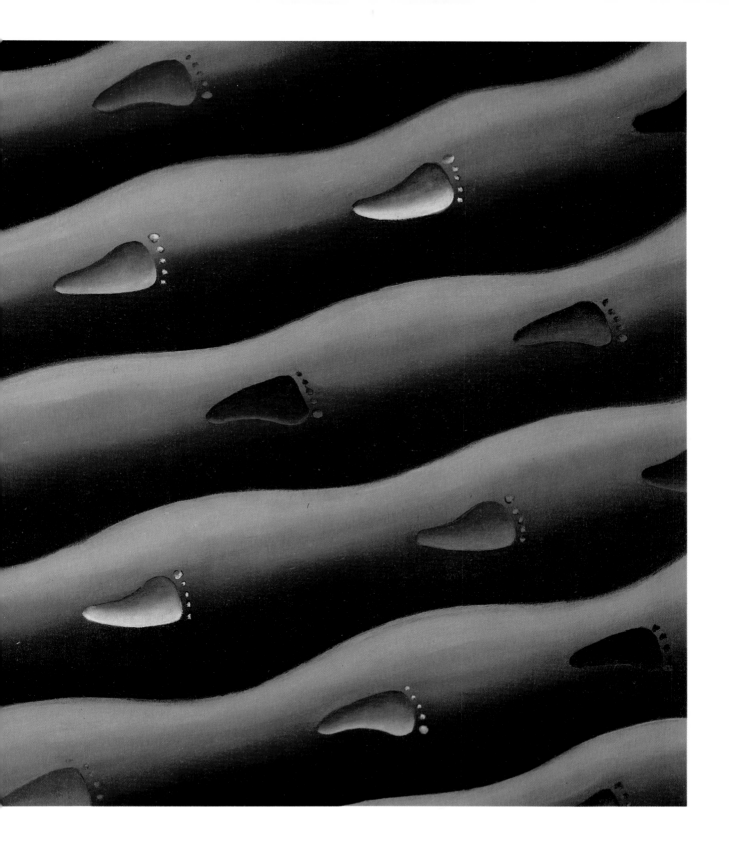

Neither the first nor the last Great Peace March.

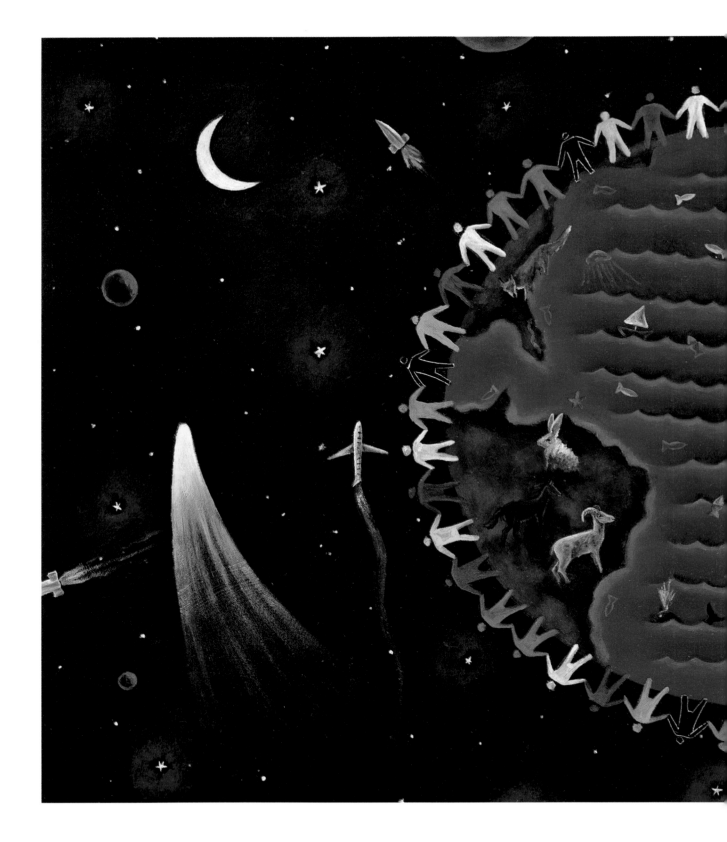

Life is a great and mighty march!

Forever, for love and for life on the Great Peace March.

The Great Peace March

Words and Music by HOLLY NEAR

An- cient eyes are watch-ing in the night The stars come out to guide the way The
Are you black like night or red like clay Are you gold like sun or brown like earth

sun still shines des - pite the clouds And the dawn is dusk is dawn is dusk is day
Gray like mist or white like moon My love for you is the rea - son for my birth

Far- mers rise and dream to feed the world The world a-wakes to feed the heart
Peace can start with just one heart From a small step to leaps and bounds

Hearts beat while a thou-sand flags are wav-ing And the far - mer sees a dream has played a
A 'walk be-comes a race for time And a brave child calls out from the

A Note on the Great Peace March

In 1986 hundreds of people walked across the United States in the Great Peace March for Nuclear Disarmament. They marched through deserts, across rivers, and over mountains. They marched in the rain and snow and blistering heat. They marched all the way from Los Angeles to Washington, D.C. They marched because they believed that real people talking to each other can make a difference to the future of our world.

The Great Peace March wasn't the first of its kind. It followed in the footsteps of many who went before. Mahatma Gandhi led marches as part of his nonviolence campaign for the liberation of his country; Native Americans marched for land rights and cultural respect; Martin Luther King, Jr., and thousands of civil-rights activists marched for freedom; Mother Jones marched for the protection of workers and their children. Vietnam veterans, gay men and lesbians, farmers, and women have all placed one foot in front of the other, taken one step at a time to make their position in the world known—to create a path of footsteps in which others could follow.

There's an expression that goes "to walk your talk." What it means is to put your body where your mouth is—to say what you think and to act consistently with your beliefs. No matter who you are, you can find footsteps you admire, put your feet down, and move forward, taking the next step for love and for life.

That's why I wrote this song. It expresses how I feel about peace, and helps me have the courage to stand up for the things I believe in—to be part of the Great Peace March.

—Holly Near